Little Quack's
Bedtime

by **Lauren Thompson**   *pictures by* **Derek Anderson**

Simon & Schuster Books for Young Readers

NEW YORK   LONDON   TORONTO   SYDNEY

Mama Duck had five little ducklings, Widdle, Waddle, Piddle, Puddle, and Little Quack.

Day was done, and Mama Duck said,
"Snuggle close, and shut your eyes.
It's sleepy time, little ducklings!"

So Widdle, Waddle, Piddle, Puddle, and Little Quack snuggled close to Mama. Then her five little ducklings saw *blink! blink! blink!*

"Look, Mama, look!" they cried. "What's that flashing in the dark?"

Mama Duck looked, and then she said,
"Those are fireflies winking 'good night.'
That's what is blinking in the dark.
Now it's sleepy time, little ducklings."

Widdle shut her eyes and went to sleep.
But Waddle, Piddle, Puddle, and Little
Quack were still awake.
Those four little ducklings heard
whooo! whooo! whooo!
"Listen, Mama, listen!" they cried.
"What's that hooting in the dark?"

Mama Duck listened, and then she said,
"That's an owl perched high above.
That's what is hooting in the dark.
Now it's sleepy time, little ducklings."

Waddle shut his eyes and went to sleep.
But Piddle, Puddle, and Little Quack were still awake.
Those three little ducklings saw something
sway, sway, sway.
"Look, Mama, look!" they cried. "What's that moving
in the dark?"

Mama looked, and then she said,
"That's the tree that you play beside.
That's what is moving in the dark.
Now it's sleepy time, little ducklings."

Then Piddle shut her eyes and went to sleep.
But Puddle and Little Quack were still awake.
Those two little ducklings heard
swish! swish! swish!
"Listen, Mama, listen!" they cried.
"What's that rustling in the dark?"

Mama Duck listened, and then she said,
"Those are the reeds saying 'hush' to the night.
That's what is rustling in the dark.
Now it's sleepy time, little ducklings."

Puddle shut his eyes and went to sleep.
But Little Quack was still awake.
Little Quack looked. Little Quack listened.
All around was *dark, dark, dark.*

"Mama!" he cried. "Why, oh, why is the night so dark?"

Mama snuggled close, and then she said,
"So the stars can shine their twinkling light.
That's why the night is, oh, so dark.
Now it's sleepy time, little duckling."

Then Little Quack shut his eyes . . .
and went to sleep. . . .

Good night, little ducklings, good night!

Sweet dreams, Cheryl
—D. A.

To Owen, our snuggly
little duckling—L. T.

SIMON & SCHUSTER BOOKS FOR YOUNG READERS

An imprint of Simon & Schuster Children's Publishing Division

1230 Avenue of the Americas, New York, New York 10020

Text copyright © 2005 by Lauren Thompson

Illustrations copyright © 2005 by Derek Anderson

All rights reserved, including the right of reproduction in whole or in part in any form.

SIMON & SCHUSTER BOOKS FOR YOUNG READERS is a trademark of Simon & Schuster, Inc.

Book design by Greg Stadnyk

The text for this book is set in Stone Informal.

The illustrations for this book are rendered in acrylic on canvas.

Manufactured in China

2 4 6 8 10 9 7 5 3 1

CIP data for this book is available from the Library of Congress.

ISBN 0-689-86894-4

first
edition